Margo

Anna Yosifova

Margo

Vanguard Press

VANGUARD PAPERBACK

© Copyright 2024
Anna Yosifova

The right of Anna Yosifova to be identified as author of
this work has been asserted by her in accordance with the
Copyright, Designs and Patents Act 1988.

All Rights Reserved

No reproduction, copy or transmission of this publication
may be made without written permission.
No paragraph of this publication may be reproduced,
copied or transmitted save with the written permission of the
publisher, or in accordance with the provisions
of the Copyright Act 1956 (as amended).

Any person who commits any unauthorised act in relation to
this publication may be liable to criminal
prosecution and civil claims for damages.

A CIP catalogue record for this title is
available from the British Library.

ISBN 978 1 80016 924 1

This is a work of fiction. Names, characters, businesses, places,
events and incidents are either the product of the author's imagination or
used in a fictitious manner. Any resemblance to actual persons, living or
dead, or actual events is purely coincidental.

Vanguard Press is an imprint of
Pegasus Elliot Mackenzie Publishers Ltd.
www.pegasuspublishers.com

First Published in 2024

Vanguard Press
Sheraton House Castle Park
Cambridge England

Printed & Bound in Great Britain

To my whole family, thank you!
To J for being simply the best!

1.

It was such a cold December morning. There was no sign of the sun, only big and dark clouds in the sad, gray sky. The house was quiet. Everyone was still sound asleep. Margo poured herself a big cup of coffee and took one cigarette from her emergency pack that was hidden deep in the top drawer in the kitchen. Just where she left them, she had a change of heart and placed them in her pocket. As quietly as possible she opened the old wooden door and stepped into the garden. The wind started pushing into her. She lit the cigarette and sat on the steps. 'It's just for today, Mom. I need it,' she whispered to herself and smiled.

After Rosaline's passing Margo had been feeling more lost than ever. She and her mum were more like sisters than mother and daughter. Every little gossip, every little secret was always shared between them. Their everyday conversations sometimes were as simple as, 'How are you?' or their more intense conversations that included, 'Did you know what happened today?' were never going to happen again and Margo didn't know how to feel. After the funeral, a lot of people were telling her that it is normal for her to be crying, howling and whatnot. But Margo didn't cry, scream or bawl her eyes out. She just simply felt totally and entirely lost.

The door behind her squeaked and she saw Kyle's grumpy face. He was holding his red cup filled with coffee to the brim and he sat down next to her, yawning loudly.

'You realize it's six-thirty in the morning, right?'

'And you realize that there's no need for you to fill your cup to the brim, right? The coffee won't run away,' she smiled.

'Do you have another one?' he asked and pointed at her cigarette. She took the pack out of her cardigan's pocket and watched her little brother lighting the cigarette with surprise.

'Shut up,' he said and laughed. 'It's just for today.'

Kyle and Margo had a five year gap between them, but they were always mistaken for twins.

Even though Kyle was the younger one, he was taller than her. They were so similar.

From face features to characters, sometimes it made you think you're talking to the same person.

'Have you talked with Adam? Did you tell them?' he asked casually.

There was an awkward silence and then she looked up.

'I will, tonight. At dinner,' she whispered.

'Mm, do you want me to be there? To calm the situation if it gets a bit much?'

'I'm just worried how both of them will react. Rose, leaving her friends and Adam, leaving the team,' she took another cigarette out, lit it and continued, 'I'm still worried that we are making a mistake.'

'We can always come back here and you know that. But I think this will be a nice adventure for them two and for us as well. A bit of a change is not that bad. And we need it, after mum's passing and your ex-husband going off the rails. Plus, no one is going to miss New York.' Theyl aughed. 'I got you, we will be fine.' She rested her head on his shoulder and, finally, she felt a little bit of peace in her soul.

The day went by mainly cleaning the house and making her best lasagna. She had to make tonight as calm and nice as possible. She knew Rose was too little to even fully understand what was going to happen, so she was most worried about Adam. The seventeen-year-old teenager she was raising, whose hormones were worse than ever. 'You got it, Margo. It's for the best and you know that, deep breaths,' she was telling herself, when the front door opened and loudness filled the empty house. Margo turned around and picked up little Rosaline and gently placed her on the kitchen counter while the little girl was telling her about her exciting outing with her uncle to the zoo.

'Is Adam here?' Kyle asked.

'Not yet, he's still out,' Margo replied nervously. 'Monkey, go wash your hands, please. Dinner is going to be ready soon,' she kissed her forehead. The front door opened again and loud boots started walking up and down the little corridor.

'ADAM!' Rose yelled and threw herself in her big brother's arms. 'I went to the zoo today,' She started telling him.

'Sounds great, but you can tell me later, okay,' he said and placed her on the ground. 'Hey, what's up? I'm not late for dinner, am I?' he laughed.

'Nope, right on time actually. Go wash your hands.' Margo gave him half a smile and disappeared into the kitchen.

They sat down at the round table, trying to maintain a normal family picture. After Rosaline's death, except little Rose, no one had been feeling truly in the mood for smiles.

'I have some news,' Margo finally spoke, while cutting a piece of the lasagna and fighting with the melted cheese.

'What's up?'

She took a deep breath. 'I decided to move us to Stonebrake.'

Silence. Again. Thick and disgusting and seemingly it was predominant in the house the last couple of months.

'Is this because of Gavin and what happened with Rose?' he said angrily. 'I told you, I can deal with him, why are you not listening?'

'It's not only that, Adam, and you know it. He won't stop coming into our lives,' Margo replied tiredly.

'You're so selfish,' he stood up and yelled. 'Never thinking about OUR lives, but, hey, it was already decided, right! Moving me and Rose in the middle of the school year is probably the worst idea you ever had.' The boy left the table and ran out of the door. Kyle stood up ready to follow him, but Margo grabbed his shoulder stopping him.

'No,' she waved her hand and went after him.

It was snowing outside. A cold January night. The snow quickly covered Margo's dark hair, she knew exactly where to find Adam, so she paced quickly through the empty street right until the end of it. And here he was, pacing in one place in the corner.

He looked at her unbelievably and hesitated for a second. 'I used to be your age too, you know. I had the same fears and worries as you.' She stared at her son, her baby who wasn't a baby anymore. He was a man; brave and strong. 'Adam, I know how you feel. But after everything that happened with your father and Rose and then your grandma's passing. I can't... I... ' He placed his arm around her shoulders and hugged her tight.

'I know,' he whispered.

'I just need to protect you two, and I can't do that here,' her voice was more like a whisper.

Adam breathed deeply and looked at her.

'Okay, then. But just because I'm agreeing with that, it doesn't mean I'm happy about it, because I'm not. I hate it. But we will move. But, first, you need to make a promise.'

She focused her eyes on him.

'After I finish high school, you need to let me come back to New York,' his voice was now serious.

'You are no longer a little boy,' she murmured. 'Let's go home, I'm freezing,' she said loudly.

Maybe it will be okay, she thought to herself or maybe prayed.

After they finished dinner, Adam read two chapters of "Harry Potter and the Prisoner of Azcaban" to Rose who fell asleep almost immediately after. He went back to his room and sat on his bed. The blue sheets had been in a ball in the corner since this morning. A lot was going through his head. He did accept the fact that they are moving in his own way and he did agree to an extent it will be a good way to start again. It's not like he had anyone stopping him from moving anyway. He lost all his friends, his girlfriend broke up with him last week, stating "you have changed and are now unrecognizable." Had he though? In a way, he felt more mature than anything else. His whole view of the world has changed. He lay down on the bed placing his hands behind his neck. He tried imagining his new life and then she popped up. Heather. His godmother's daughter. There's no escape from her. He thought back to that one summer they spent together two years ago. His first love. The night before he left for New York they made love for the first time in their short lives. He slept with other girls after that, not many, of course, he wasn't that kind of guy but nothing matched her, nothing came even close to her and her kindred spirit. Only she saw Adam, the real him full with fears and dreams. He wished he could change everything that happened after, he regretted not reaching out to her but it was too late now. He turned on his left side, trying to push the thoughts away but her face was all he was seeing, even with his eyes closed.

2.

The house was now full of boxes but felt empty. Full of memories that shouldn't be remembered.

'Hey, we are ready!' Kyle said behind Margo. She looked around her and smiled.

'Adam took his first steps on the stairs here. And Rose said her first word while looking at herself in the mirror here,' she laughed. Silence, barely breathable, again. 'This house used to be a happy place, safe place. What happened?' she whispered more to herself. 'Let's go!'

It was going to take around ten hours for them to land and reach their final destination. Margo didn't even realize how much she missed England. The last time she was here, she spent no more than twelve hours in total and she wasn't in her right mind, taking care of her mother's funeral and making sure the house was secure enough for the long run; she couldn't feel any other feeling than pure sadness. Adam was with his headphones for the whole flight and they were probably glued to his ears by now, he knew that what his family was doing was the right thing to do, at least for Rose's sake. And he knew that soon he would be able to go back to New York. Just a couple of months away. Rose just kept asking questions and requesting stories from her mother and uncle's childhood. Margo was listening to her brother's calming voice about their little adventures in the garden or their family walks on the beach and, for a second, she let herself go back in time to memories long forgotten. And just for a second, she was seven again, running barefoot after their old golden retriever, Betsy.

***

The car stopped on 'Old Valley Street'. The house and front door were painted in a bright yellow and beige color and was two floors big. The windows were deep brown; Margo's favorite color.

The garden that their parents used to spend hours in was now full of wildflowers and the beautiful white roses that were her mother's pride and joy were long in the past. The big oak tree in the backyard was the same ugly and big tree as she remembered it.

'Okay, boys and Rose, there're three bedrooms so, for now, Rose and I are gonna share a room until we turn the basement into a bedroom for Adam. How does that sound?' Margo asked.

The living room was half covered in white and blue sheets placed there by her after her mom's death. Who would've guessed a couple of months later the house was awake once more? Filled with old memories, half of them long forgotten and new ones soon to be made. Rose's little giggles, Adam's teenage drama, Margo and Kyle's little conversations, spoken in secret.

Everything was left as she remembered. The bright red sofa that kept so many sleepovers and gossip. The wooden coffee table that was made by her father was now uncovered waiting for the next book to be put on top of it. The big, old bookshelf that covered most of the wall was full with her parents' favorite books and, here and there, you can find Margo's books left there for someone to find. She picked up an old copy of 'Greek Mythology' by Nikolay Kun and opened the fragile, yellow pages. On the first page was her name written with big letters. Time has taken its toll on this book, but the smell of it still made Margo's heart jump with happiness.

The long journey from New York took its toll on everyone but Margo, who was more awake than ever. Her mind was rushing, her heart felt like it was exploding.

'Mom!' Adam's voice echoed in the room. Margo jumped, her eyes wide open.

'Did you sleep on the sofa? You weirdo!' Kyle laughed. 'I couldn't sleep,' she answered.

'I had the big bed ALL for myself.' Rose was jumping up and down on the sofa leaving Margo no choice but to get up.

The rest of the week went past in a blink of an eye. After receiving everything from their old home in New

York, Margo finally managed to put their new home under some kind of control until there was no trace of the boxes. The basement was freshly painted in a nice dark gray color by Adam, who immediately moved downstairs. Rose took Margo's old room which still had her old daisy-painted walls and her old fluffy toys. Kyle took his old room which was now painted dark blue and threw away his posters from the wall so it looked like a half-decent room for an adult. Margo took her parent's old room that she hated so much while growing up, but now she was afraid to even touch anything in this room. The picture from her parent's wedding was still sitting on the wooden dresser. She carefully put her mother's jewelry in a small box and tucked them in one of the suitcases that were almost full of old clothes left by Rosaline.

'Hey, how's it going?' Kyle knocked on the door.

'It's... going,' she laughed. 'You know, I think mom was a hoarder.' She laughed even harder.

'She kept dad's torn socks and, while cleaning the basement, I found our old school books.'

'Well, mom was special! Anyway, I'm taking Adam to the school so we can give his last documents, wanna join us?' he asked.

'As nice as it sounds, no. I have so much more to do in the house and Evelyn and Heather are coming for dinner tonight so I need to cook. Can you go to the store after?'

'Oh my. Evie and Margo together again? God saves us all.' A pillow flew and hit him right in the face, which made Kyle laugh hysterically.

The evening was very special for Margo. She and Evelyn were best friends since first grade, skipping classes together, smoking their first cigarette together, and crushing on the same actors. If Evie was there, Margo was there too! Adam and Heather were born just a couple of weeks apart.

And Margo and Evie were only eighteen, which was absolute madness for most people, but for them two it was another special thing in their life. It was definitely not planned but it was another path to walk together. Although Margo's marriage went down the drain, Evelyn was still going strong with her high school sweetheart. They kept their friendship strong, even with the distance.

Kyle parked the car right in front of the school.

'Do you want to come with me or are you going to stay in the car?' he asked Adam.

He didn't answer, just removed his seatbelt and got out of the car. His expression was dead.

'So are you excited for tomorrow?' Kyle asked.

'No!' he answered and opened the door. Kyle laughed for a second and followed him inside.

The school walls were freshly painted but everything else was old. A big wall full of trophies caught Adam's attention.

'Go, Stonebrake,' his uncle whispered and smiled. 'Back in the day, the team was amazing. We won so many trophies there was barely a space for the new ones. I'm sure you got your love for football from me.' His left hand was now resting on his shoulder. 'I'm sure there'll be tryouts for the team the first week. Why don't you try?'

Adam was quiet for a minute.

'Because I play American football!' Adam's voice sounded almost offended.

'You have played with me more times than I can even remember.'

'Doesn't matter, it's not my sport or team for that matter.' He shut down the subject and started looking around the school corridor.

'Have you spoken with Victor since the incident?' Kyle asked carefully, wording his question.

'No,' Adam replied and walked off.

Margo was preparing the dinner when the bell rang. She rushed to open the door and Evelyn was standing there in her glory. Her long blonde hair was in a tight bun and her arms were spread out waiting for a hug, one hand holding tightly onto a bottle of white wine.

'It's been so long since the last day I was in this house.' She looked around, her fingers touching everything around her, smiling at the memories that were flowing in her head.

'Are Heather and Ned joining us?' Margo asked while placing the plates on the table.

'She should be on her way now, she has some things to do in school and Ned is working late shifts at work. Can you believe that the kids are actually graduating? It's crazy,' she said.

'Adam and Kyle are at the school, to hand in last-minute documents. Do you want me to give them a call so they can take her with them?' Margo offered and took her phone.

'That sounds great, she can be so slow to come from point A to point B sometimes,' Evie laughed.

Kyle put back his phone in his pocket and walked out of the principal's office.

'Your mom just called saying that Evelyn is at home, but Heather is apparently at school. Let me give her a call.'

Adam looked at him a bit scared and shocked.

'Heather?' he repeated.

'Isn't that her?' he asked and pointed at the exit door. She had changed. She was taller and her hair shorter, but still a black raven color.

Adam wanted to hide and not show his face ever again. After the last time they saw each other, they didn't end things on the best note or even a good one for that matter. After three years, he had been anxious to see her. Every day at school for at least six months.

'Uncle Kyle?' she said loudly, her voice echoing in the empty corridor.

'Heather, oh, my God, look at you,' he gave her a tight hug. Her smile disappeared when she saw Adam.

'Adam. Hi,' she murmured and he only nodded, trying to avoid looking at her as much as possible.

'Come on, kids. Let's get home, I'm starving.'

It was pouring with rain outside, but inside the house was boiling hot. Maybe it was the wine or the company or maybe even both. Heather and Adam were sitting in silence listening to their parents recalling old and ancient stories. Kyle was all red from the heat and his blonde hair was an absolute mess, but he couldn't stop laughing with Margo and Evelyn.

'Oh, God, I missed you two so much,' Eve said through tears. She wiped them with her hand and took a sip from her wine glass. 'Kyle, I took it upon myself to speak with Mr. Green, the principal of Stonebrake School; they have been in dire need of new teachers since last year and I know you really like being a PE teacher so I offered you to him. He agreed to meet with you next week to see how it goes from there if you are available, of course.'

Kyle smiled so brightly, he could light a thousand candles. 'I would love to.'

The night went by fast and, before they knew it, Evelyn and Heather had to head home. It was a brief look exchanged between Heather and Adam that made Margo remember that there was something between the two kids, long forgotten, or maybe it wasn't.

3.

The first day in a new school was scary for Adam. The boy with anger issues. He was giving himself a day for everyone to find out what had happened back in New York and to be judged.

He knew what to expect so he didn't have a lot of hope for at least a decent year at the school.

'Give me a call when you finish school today and if you want you can come to the shop and give me a hand, okay?' Margo said. Her son was deep in his thoughts and everything that was said to him was long forgotten seconds after. He put his headphones on and waved his hand goodbye.

'Are you worried about him?' Kyle asked.

Margo took the half-eaten plate from the table and threw the eggs in the bin.

'I am,' she replied calmly. 'What if they know one of the reasons for our move? What if they treat him differently or he is being bullied or something?'

'Sis, have you seen Adam lately? He's a big boy, he can take care of himself plus he will never let anyone bully him, you will see.'

Even if it wasn't snowing, the weather was still cold and foggy. But this kind of weather was Margo's favorite. It was calming and somehow worth loving. Rose was the only person in their family who was free of any anxiety or worries. Just a carefree child who was looking forward to making new friends. The only person that Margo wasn't worried about that she won't get used to the new town and its perks.

The little girl gave her mum a big kiss on the cheek, boldly let go of her hand and, without turning back, she started talking with her new teacher, who now had her small hand in hers. Mrs. Shaw was a lovely middle-aged lady who just adored kids. So Margo wasn't worried at all, because she knew that the teacher would take great care of her, not so little anymore, girl. The next stop was her mom's shop. She parked the car right in front of it and, before leaving, she had a quick look at it. The windows were covered in paper. The yellow sign on top of the shop saying 'Rose's Secrets' was so rusty you could barely read it. Everything was full of dust and memories. In the back room, there were boxes full of handmade jewelry.

'So, are you sure you want to turn this place into a diner?' her brother asked. He touched one of the stands and his fingertip filled with dust.

'I mean, I don't see myself making and selling jewelry, you know. 'Margo had to shout so Kyle could hear her. She tried reaching for one of the boxes from the top shelf, when the box tore above her head. Her hair which was made in a perfect bun on the top of her head was now full of little fake diamonds that fell all over the sticky floor.

'I really think we need at least another hand with this,' Kyle said, looking at the mess.

'You think!' Margo replied with dissatisfaction. 'Dad's truck,' she murmured. 'When will it be ready?'

'Simon said he will give me a call at the end of the day. It was something quite minor so it will be fixed tomorrow at the latest.'

Margo's old jeep managed to fit most of the boxes, but not all of them. They threw away so many things but, every time they thought half of the job was done, tsomething else popped out. She kept looking at her watch so she wouldn't miss her appointment with the construction guy who was going to help her rebuild the place.

A couple of hours later, Margo opened the door of the little café and was pleasantly surprised to see how many people were inside. It gave her hope for her own diner. The table that was facing the big windows was occupied by a man in his 30s. His hair was hidden under a green and yellow cap. He saw Margo and stood up with a big smile.

'Margo Hunter?' he asked and held out his left arm ready to shake.

He was at least a head and a half taller than her. His jeans were stained with different colors of paint and his green t-shirt showed his body muscles. Margo had been single since her divorce was finalized six years ago. Since then, she never dated or even met anyone who was good enough for her and her kids.

'Yes. It's nice to meet you, Mr. Delaney,' she shook his hand and smiled brightly.

'Please call me Luke.' He pointed to the chair next to him and they sat down.

Somehow, for the first time in a really long time, Margo thought about how she looked; was she sweaty or covered in dust? She tried to push the thoughts to the side but she just blankly stared at him.

'Oh, you have something on your hair,' he laughed and pointed. She tried to reach it, but couldn't find it. 'Here.' he took out a little diamond from her bun. Her cheeks turned bright red.

'Like I already told you, we definitely need more help to clean that shop,' she laughed.

The meeting took three-and-a-half-hours and four coffees each. She tried to stick to her budget, which was more than enough to cover everything. Finally, her dream was close to happening.

Her phone rang and took them from their trance that they had been under for the past few of hours.

'I can't believe the time,' she said, surprised.

'Well, I believe we went through the main things. I will work on the plans tonight and will send you more information tomorrow morning and, if you're free, I would like to have another look at the place. How does that sound?'

'Yes, absolutely. I am free after nine tomorrow. Can we meet in front?' She placed her phone in her back pocket and extended her hand for a shake. He grabbed it and smiled.

'Okay, then. It's a date,' he laughed.

4.

After another almost sleepless night, Margo was getting ready for the new day. But this morning, she took an extra effort to get ready. A bit of makeup here and there, a sweater that didn't have holes i it. She felt silly, but she still did it anyway.

Adam was almost hugging his cup of coffee, while talking with Rose about the flowers that were over the little window above the sink. Before entering the kitchen, she stopped and quietly observed their innocent conversation and, as usual, Rose was chatting away.

'Let me ask you something, do you like your school?'' she asked with a serious tone. His body slumped onto the chair next to hers.

'I don't know yet,' he simply replied. 'But I do miss my friends back in New York.'

'It's okay, Adam. I am your friend anyway.' She gave him a little kiss on the cheek and continued talking about the flowers. The relationship between the two siblings was always so sacred and pure. Even though there was a big age gap, they could understand each other with just a look.

Margo stood next to the door listening to their conversation. A feeling of guilt crashed into her chest. The last year of high school should be special, something to remember, and creating memories for life. Maybe she made a mistake moving him so far away.

''Morning, Mom,' Adam said.

'Good morning, my chickens. Where's Kyle?' she asked while pouring herself a cup of coffee.

'He had to leave early for school. It's his first day and he told me he's scared,' Rose laughed.

When the kids were safely left at school, Margo drove to the shop; she was sweaty and anxious.

'Stop doing that! He probably has a family and wife. You are so naive, Margo.' She gave herself a quick pep-talk and parked in front. Luke was waiting outside the shop. He was looking through the dirty windows. When she got out of the car she realized he was holding two takeaway cups of coffee.

'Mr. Delaney,' she greeted him.

'Please, I said to call me Luke,' he smiled and gave her her cup.

'Oh, thank you,' she blushed. 'Shall we?' She unlocked the door and let some fresh air inside the shop, soon to be a diner.

Luke started walking around and touching the floorboards with his boots. The walls were full of cracks and his hand moved around, touching them gently. His face was serious and unfazed. The weather was really cold but he was just wearing a shirt and Margo let herself have a look at him.

'Okay, I am going to be really real with you. This place is in awful shape. If I were you I would sell it and use the money to buy a new place,' he was squatting down next to one of the walls.

'But I can see it is a very sentimental place to you, huh?

'It used to be my mom's shop. She passed away a couple of months ago,' she replied.

'Oh, I see.'

'I know it might take longer than what we talked about but it's really important for me to stay within the budget because I can't really afford to go above it. Every saved penny is here!' she had this concerned look on her face and a vein in her forehead popped up.

'I will try my best, Margo!' he replied and gave her a genuine smile that made her legs a bit shaky. 'Can I ask you something?' his tone changed drastically. 'My friend is opening a new restaurant with delicious seafood next week. I was wondering... whether you would like to go... with me?'

'Of course, I am not entirely sure if you are single, but as I don't see a ring and all I thought... '

Margo froze for a split second. Was he inviting her on a date or was it a friendly dinner?

'Erm... I am... divorced, but... I'm not sure if that's a great idea,' she replied awkwardly. 'I mean, we work together and I think it might make things a bit weird… '

'Okay, then. We can make it a friend date!' he laughed. 'It's gonna be just two adult people trying a new restaurant. How about that?'

'Okay!' she heard herself saying.

Margo's phone rang, she excused herself and went outside.

'Mrs. Hunter?' a male voice questioned.

'I am she.'

'I am calling regarding your son, Adam. Unfortunately, he was in a fight and, well, I think it's best for you to come to the school to talk and then take him home.'

Right this second she realized history was repeating itself. She took a deep breath and went inside.

'Something happened at my son's school. I… I have to go,' her voice was shaky. She felt dizzy.

"For fuck sake… " she said to herself.

Luke was looking at her with affection. A strange feeling he hadn't felt in a long time towards a woman.

'If you want, I can call my guys to come and have a look at the electricity because that is most important, while you go and take care of him. Leave the keys with me and come later to pick them up. What do you say?' He was smiling. A genuine smile.

'I… I don't know what to say. Thank you.' She was grateful.

'Don't worry about it, I have two boys myself. I know the struggle. You have my number, call me when you're on your way.'

The principal's office was dark. Everything in the room was in dark mahogany, which gave her the creeps. Kyle and Margo absorbed every word that the old man was saying, while Adam was staring at his bloody knuckles.

'I understand that he was pushed into this fight by things that were said by the other boy but, officially, Adam was the first to throw the punch. I think two weeks suspension and three weeks in detention will do him well. Giving him time to think about what he did.' The principal's face was exhausted, angry, and disappointed. The same feelings were flowing through Margo's body but, right now, her anger was stronger than the rest.

'Thank you, Mr. Green. I'm sure Adam feels deep remorse about what happened and I will make sure it does not happen again.'

The office's door squeaked. In the corridor, Heather was waiting for them. Next to her, was sitting the other boy, who had been in the fight. He was holding a napkin on his nose, but the blood was still streaming down his face. Margo's heart started beating even faster.

Heather stood up and opened her mouth to say something but Adam was faster.

'I am not surprised you told them you know, I was even surprised that it took you so long,' His voice was angry, his hands were now in tight fists. He gave her a last look and started walking away.

'Go to class, Heather,' Kyle ordered her.

Adam was just like Margo. Since he was a kid, everyone knew that the resemblance between both characters was undeniable. He was easy to talk to when he was in the mood but, God, he had real anger issues, just like his mother. And when anger took over them both, nothing could stop them from exploding.

'Where are we going?' he asked.

'Don't you dare talk right now, or I swear I'm going to stop the car, kick you out and you can walk to the house,' she said.

'It wasn't my fault,' he said with a calm tone, even though he wanted to shout.

Margo parked the car in front of the shop and unbuckled her seat belt. She turned around so she could face him.

'What the hell is your problem, boy?' she yelled.

'They all knew what had happened in New York,' he tried saying calmly, but his blood was boiling from inside.

'YOU BROKE THE BOY'S NOSE, ADAM. YOU'RE LUCKY HE DOESN'T SUE YOU.'

Margo was shaking with anger. She took a deep breath.

'Adam, I understand that what has happened is too heavy for you. It might even suffocate you sometimes, but you can't let this eat you alive because, right now, it is ruining your life. You talked with the therapist, I tried reaching out to you, Kyle tried talking to you, but you just kept pushing us away. Violence is not the answer.'

'I regret what I did... back home,' his voice was now low. He sounded like a lost baby.'I almost killed my own father.'

Margo was taken aback for a second. This was the first time he said these words out loud.

'Then I almost beat my best friend to death,' he stopped. His eyes were tearful. His mother wasn't sure what to do. She grabbed his hand and hugged him tightly.

'You did what you had to at that moment, you saved your sister,' she took his face in her hands.

'The situation got out of hand, but you can always reach out to Victor. You can own up to your mistakes.'

He shook his head and wiped his face with his jacket. He knew he had to do something. He had to talk with Victor.

5.

Kyle's life was a big roller coaster. His relationships were no longer than two to three months. His only relationship that was longer than that was with crazy Thalia. The only girl that managed to keep him for that long, but it wasn't easy. All the yelling and throwing things at him, all the cheating accusations. Her nickname was true down to every single bit. But he loved her, even though she had a place in a mental hospital. His decision to leave New York was tough and quite easy at the same time. He wanted a new start and he wasn't getting any younger. But his soul was craving to be free, his heart was aching for love. Rosaline's death was quite the wake-up call for both him and Margo. It made him realize that life is short and that it should be lived to the fullest. So him moving to Stonebrake was his way of showing himself that, whatever is supposed to happen, will happen and not to look for it, but to wait for it to find you. Whatever it was. And in the meantime, just live the life that you want.

And he lived by this every day for months now and, on his first day of the new job, there she was. A woman whose smile was so bright, it hit him like a wave in the ocean. A feeling that was barely recognizable floated through him, his stomach was tight. He couldn't stop staring at her.

For him, she was the most beautiful girl he had ever seen. Her long brown hair was in a high ponytail. She was wearing just a simple pair of black jeans and a black and white blouse. Her eyes were bright blue. And for the rest of the day, he regretted not going there to say one simple 'hello'. His first day went by fast. Meeting the students and some of the teachers made him a bit overwhelmed and brought him lots of memories from his old school. But even after everything that happened with Adam, he didn't let that ruin his day.

It was pouring after school. A lightning storm, his favorite. The moment he exited the doors, he saw her again. She was sitting in front of the door, trying to open her umbrella. And just like that, the open-minded Kyle, the guy who could sweet-talk every girl into anything he wanted, disappeared. And a total stranger took his place. She turned around and smiled.

'Horrible storm, innit?!' Her American accent was so noticeable and took him by surprise. He gave her a half-smile and the door closed behind him. She obviously gave up on her umbrella and shoved it in her bag. 'You must be Kyle Henderson. I was meaning to come today to meet you, but time flew so fast. My name is Eleanor Roberts, I am the school counselor.' Her hands were flying in the air when she talked, making her more cute.

'It's okay, I accept your apology,' he joked. 'Erm... would you like a ride?' he heard himself offering.

'That would be so sweet of you, but I don't want to...

'Don't be silly,' he stopped her. 'Do you see the blue car just over there?' he pointed to the end of the parking lot. 'On three, we run to it and pray we won't get too wet.' Her smile was big and generous, giving Kyle butterflies in his stomach.

Adam was sitting on the kitchen stool, staring at his phone, mainly at his chat with Victor. The last thing written was months ago about a football practice they were gonna go to. To him it felt like yesterday. He really missed his best friend, who was not his best friend anymore. More like the person who knew him best, but was pushed away by him. And it was rightly so.

'Is that Vic? Say hi from me,' Rose's voice rang in his ears, bringing him back to Earth.

The front door opened and closed. Kyle was all wet making big and muddy footprints behind himself in the hallway.

'You're really late, huh,' Adam laughed. 'Where were you?'

Kyle took off his jacket. 'You disappointed me so much today, I'm not ready to talk normally and be friendly with you yet,' he said and left the kitchen. Rose laughed, which scored her an angry look from Adam.

'Hey, you!' Kyle said to Margo and sat on the bed next to her. She turned her tablet to him and showed him her painting of her dream diner.

'Oh wow, that looks amazing!' The counter was dark mahogany and the tables were in the same color but a deeper and richer brown. For the chairs, Margo decided to go for dark burgundy. The walls were freshly painted in a honey color with gorgeous vintage paintings in the corner in boxes waiting to be put on the walls.

'It has a "sophisticated forest" vibe,' Kyle said. 'It reminds me of "Gilmore Girls",' he continued.

'If you start singing the theme song I'm going to kick you out of the house,' Margo laughed.

'Why are you so late anyway?'

'Well, I gave a lift to one of my colleagues. It was pouring outside,' he replied. 'It's actually a she. And she is really sweet.'

Margo raised her eyebrows in dismay.

'Nothing will happen though, she is my colleague and that can get really nasty really fast,' his tone was somehow sad. Even though he knew her for only twenty minutes, he really wanted to get to know her.

'Never say never!' she whispered.

'If you start singing Justin Bieber I'm going to kick you out of the house.' They both started laughing and Margo placed her head on his shoulder.

***

Evelyn held the color sample above her head. A beautiful pastel shade of purple. Her favorite color. She had a good look at it and gave it to Margo who did the same as her friend.

'Do you think Heather is having sex?' Margo asked casually.

'I hope not. I mean she hasn't said anything to me, but she's been in a relationship with this guy, Zack for a couple of months now.' Eve made a disgusted face when she mentioned the boy's name.

'You really don't like him, huh?'

'God, no! Every time I see his face I really want to smack him but he hasn't given me a reason yet.' Margo laughed.

'When we were her age your body count was six plus.'

'Don't remind me, please. Oh, look at that color.' She passed Margo a shade of white.

'No, too bright. I will have to paint over it every two weeks,' she explained. 'I mean Adam did tell me when he slept with a girl for the first time, but that was a long time ago so it makes me wonder... '

'Honey, they are teenagers. Whoever keeps saying kids don't have sex is lying to themselves.'

All we can do is talk about it with them and make sure they do it safely. The first time I mentioned it, Heather couldn't look me in the eyes for a week.' They giggled.

'I'm going out with Luke Delaney!' Margo said fast and started walking away.

'The architect, Luke Delaney? The one who is helping you with the diner?' her voice made a squeaky noise. 'When are you going?'

'Tomorrow.' Margo avoided eye contact.

'Oh my. We need to go shopping.'

'No.' She smiled at Eve and grabbed a pink towel from the stand.

Evelyn grabbed the towel and threw it back in its place. She took her hand and started walking out of the shop.

'We are definitely going shopping!' she replied without giving her another chance to say no.

Back at home, Adam was watching the football game on the sofa trying not to overthink his entire life, again. The bell rang. He groaned loudly and opened the door. To his surprise it was Heather. The last person that he was expecting.

'Can I come in?' she asked and walked into the house.

'Help yourself,' he said sarcastically. 'What do you want?'

She was nervous, anxious. Her hands clasped together tightly. 'I honestly didn't mean this to happen. I thought… '

'You thought nothing, as per usual. We haven't talked in a year and from nowhere you think you know me,' his voice was now angry. 'Just stop pretending you're my friend because you're not.'

'I'm not pretending anything, I really care about you.' Her heart was pounding.

Adam was even more angry now. He placed his hand on the wall above her head pinning her body on the cold cement.

'I don't care about you,' he whispered. His face was so close to hers.

'You're not the only one who got hurt that day, Adam.' She gazed into his deep brown eyes. 'Just because you left, it doesn't mean our feelings left too.' Her soft hand brushed his cheek before he pushed his body away from her. 'I am trying to be your friend, but you're making it unnecessarily hard!' The door closed behind her, leaving Adam confused. She opened old wounds that he didn't even know he had.

6.

Margo looked at herself in the old mirror that was hanging on the wall. The dress that Evelyn found was in a dark navy blue color. Her short hair was falling freely on her shoulders, her arms touched the satin. She felt beautiful. A feeling that was long forgotten. Sometimes she even forgot she was human. She put on a bit of mascara and some lipstick.

Kyle and Adam were playing poker at the table while Rose was occupying the tv.

'Oh, wow, you look dazzling for a 'friend' date.' Kyle smiled.

'Mommy, it's cold outside, take a jacket.' Rose's tiny hands wrapped around Margo's legs for a split second before running back to her spot on the sofa. She grabbed her coat, unsure whether she should go or not. A light was coming from the driveway. She pushed the curtain slightly and noticed his car outside.

'Screw it,' she whispered to herself. 'I won't be late!' she yelled and left.

The restaurant was based close to the port. It was surrounded by more restaurants, but this one was more eye-catching with its blinking lights outside and gorgeous colors inside. It was striking from afar. Orange and dark green were the main colors. So fancy and simple at the same time.

Margo was impressed and she could not stop looking around trying to breathe in every detail. The first half hour went on deciding what to eat from the menu.

Margo took a sip of her wine.

'So, tell me more about yourself,' she heard herself asking. Luke glanced at her and smiled.

'What do you want to know?'

'Anything… everything.' She studied his face. His green eyes had this wonderful spark in them and every time he smiled, his dimples showed.

'Well, I have been divorced for over three years now, I have two boys, who are absolute nightmares because of puberty. I was born and raised here. My life is quite boring to be honest.' His laugh took Margo out of the trance that his words had put her in.

'That sounds… so normal.' She poured herself more wine and took a big sip from it. 'Mine is far from normal.'

'Tell me about it.'

'Well, my youngest is obsessed with fire so I might be raising a psychopath and Adam,… ,well he is a good boy but he has really bad anger issues. My brother was supposed to be the normal one… but all hope is gone!' she laughed.

'How about your husband?' Luke asked.

'You would've known if I had one of those.'

After two bottles of wine, they decided the cold weather outside was amazing for a walk. The streets were almost empty, restaurants and cafés closing. But they didn't notice any of that, instead they were laughing so hard, they couldn't even breathe properly.

'Tell me about your wife. You promised you would after we finished that bottle of wine.'

She looked up and noticed the grin on his face. Like a flashback going through his head.

'Well… ' he started. 'Since she was a little girl she was fighting many mental illnesses; she had very bad paranoia and bipolar disorder. It was challenging, but I handled it. Until one day she was in a car crash, nothing serious, but she got worse. She started hiding her pills, lying that she'd taken them and then she would scream at the boys because she couldn't even recognise them.'

'So I didn't really have a choice but to send her to a hospice. That happened almost five years ago.'

'She's doing so much better now and the boys visit often as well.'

Margo was listening carefully, taking in every word he spoke.

'How about you? Do you visit her?' she asked.

'I did, before. The last time was four months ago. We talked and we decided to end our marriage for the sake of our sanity. We had fallen out of love, I guess,' his voice was low and he was staring at the blinking lights of the passing cars. Margo brushed her hand against his, wanting to grab it in hers and just hold it, but, instead, she put it inside her pocket.

'Your turn,' he said a bit lightly.

She smiled at him. 'My husband... Everything was going quite well in the marriage until Rose was born. Shortly after that, he lost his job and then the next one and then he turned to the bottle and it just escalated from there. He was never violent, but he became rude and absent. Coming home from time to time. Until one night he tried to... he grabbed me by the arm which left quite the bruise... ' she stopped talking, breathing in the cold air. 'He never came back after that night.'

'Oh, wow, Margo.' Luke stopped and looked at her face. The only light in the alley was coming from a small pub that was more than lively inside. He took a strand of hair that had fallen near her eye and pushed it to the side. 'I'm really sorry to hear that.'

'I guess we all have our troubled stories to tell,' her voice was a whisper. 'Fancy a pint?' she pointed at the pub behind her. 'If you want to know more of my story you will need to get me properly drunk,' she laughed.

After three pints each, they left the pub and started walking through the empty streets of the city.

Their laughs could be heard from afar.

'That was the lousiest joke I have ever heard' she said through tears.

'I wanted to do a stand-up comedy when I was younger, you're crushing my dreams right now.'

He touched her fingers slightly and then gently took her hand in his. 'You have the softest hand I have ever touched.' His voice was serious but warm. Margo felt her cheeks go bright red.

They kept walking in silence but still holding each other's hands.

'You never finished your story about your ex-husband,' he said.

'I don't want to ruin the night with talks about the past. I will tell you another time.' She looked at him and her eyes were bright like shooting stars.

'Well, I am probably going to go to prison if I get behind the wheel in my condition so I will call us a cab, is that okay?' he brushed his fingers on her cheek which was freezing cold. She stepped on her tiptoes and gently kissed him on the lips. He held her body and kissed her back. Margo's thoughts were running so fast in her head but she pushed them aside and just enjoyed the moment.

The cab driver stopped the car in front of her house. It was after midnight so it was dark. The yellow front door was glowing in the night. 'I will be just a second, don't leave without me,' Luke told the driver jokingly.

He opened the door for Margo and helped her out of the car.

'I had an amazing time tonight. I don't remember the last time I had a heart-to-heart conversation like this one. At this point we probably know each other's kids like our own.'

'I had a great time too.'

'We need to repeat it then! They do this car cinema from next week. It's supposed to be freezing outside, but the movie is promising. Maybe you would want to go?'

She moved her body a little bit closer to his.

'Maybe,' she laughed.

'But I will have to be honest, if we do go it would have to be a date.'

He pulled her towards him and kissed her. Hard and passionate. His arm was holding her back steady. She grabbed onto his neck. Their bodies were radiating such heat, but their souls were starving for more. The kisses became more and more intense.

'I have to go,' she whispered and ran in a rush. She jogged to the house, her cheeks blushing hard, but she couldn't stop smiling to herself. Maybe it was the wine that made her do that, even though she promised herself she wouldn't, but somehow she didn't regret it. She adored it, she was hungry for more.

She left her coat on the hanger and saw a light coming from the kitchen. She removed her heels and grabbed them with one hand.

'Kyle?' she said, surprised.

'Well, well, look who we have here,' he laughed. 'How was your night, Margo?'

'I need a cigarette.'

His laugh grew louder. He reached into his pocket and took a pack out. 'When we were kids, if you smoked after a night out it meant it was a good one,' he said proudly that he remembered it.

'See, I notice things.'

The garden door opened and the cold air hit them in the face. She took a blanket from the sofa and bent down, lighting the cigarette.

'So? What happened?'

She hesitated for a second and then closed her eyes.

'It was amazing,' her voice was half-angry, half-disappointed. 'It wasn't supposed to go like that. It was supposed to be awfully bad, maybe have an awkward silence where I would regret saying yes to it. But instead, we couldn't stop talking about my life, his life and our kids. We talked about school and our jobs. And he was so charming and funny.' She put her face in her palm. 'We kissed... twice and I liked it.'

The silence felt calming in the night.

'It's inevitable not to meet someone who feels familiar and good. You obviously felt it, because you said yes to going out with him. I think you should be happy that you met him. Who knows, maybe he will stick around and you will like it even more. The kids are growing, Margo. You don't deserve to be all alone your whole life.'

He was right, and she knew it, but she didn't want to accept it. Adam was going to university the following year and Rose was growing so much with every passing day. She took a deep breath and shook her head.

'I know,' she replied.

7.

Adam's suspension was officially over. He stepped into the school corridor and walked with a slow pace towards his locker.

'Adam?' an unfamiliar voice sounded behind him, 'Who's asking?'

The boy laughed, 'A future friend,' he replied. 'I'm Greg. We have history together. I saw you punch Derek, man, that guy deserved that since he was ten.' Greg was at least half a head shorter than Adam, but his body was strong and athletic. His hair was short, but was covered with a baseball cap. He noticed that Adam was confused. 'Anyway, I thought we could hang out sometime, you look cool enough for me, eh,' Greg laughed.

He didn't remember seeing him before, or maybe he hadn't been looking at all. Lunch came and Adam went to the canteen. The room was huge and full of kids. Everyone was whispering when they saw him, which was reminiscent of what happened two weeks ago. He met Heather's eyes. He felt drawn to her in so many ways. She was now living in his head every minute of every day for the last couple of weeks. She was surrounded by the loudest group of people in the whole room and he noticed she felt uncomfortable.

'Adam,' he turned around towards the now familiar voice. Greg was waving at him and he approached the table. A cute looking girl was sitting next to him, her hair was in a short pixie cut. Two more boys were arguing next to them. 'Sit, man,' Greg said and pointed at the empty chair next to him. The two guys stopped fighting and looked at him with curiosity.

'That's Adam,' he said. 'That's Joel and Dean. And that's my girlfriend, Lara.'

He answered with a weak hello and sat down.

'So you're the famous Adam everyone was talking about for a whole week, huh,' Lara smiled.

Her voice sounded so polite that she could curse and it would still sound like she was in court.

'I guess,' he replied. He felt this uneasy feeling in his chest. He hated meeting new people.

'It's cool, that guy Derek deserved a good beating,' Dean said and everyone agreed with a laugh.

The more time Adam spent with them, the more he started liking them. They reminded him of his old friends back in New York. The jokes were the same, even the arguments. It turned out that Joel and Lara were twins, who looked nothing alike. It felt good to belong somewhere.

His last class with PE. He walked into the salon and looked at his surroundings. A bunch of people who he didn't recognize and then Heather. At this point, he just smiled to himself. Is the universe making some kind of joke on him for the way he acted the last time he saw her? He had to apologize, but he was unsure how to even approach her when she was surrounded by girls every single time he saw her.

They had a five-minute water break from playing volleyball when Adam noticed Heather was finally alone. He started walking towards her when he noticed another guy on the side speaking to her. As close as he was getting, he could hear they were having an argument that involved a lot of hissed and angry language from both sides.

'Leave me alone, you idiot,' she said to him, grabbing her bag and running outside. He didn't follow her but just ran in the opposite direction, pissed. Adam went back for his backpack and followed

Heather was outside in the empty corridor.

'Hey!' he yelled behind her.

She turned around and looked at Adam. 'Go back to class, I'm fine,' her voice cracked, she was crying. She opened the door in front of her and let the cold breeze hit her sweaty face.

Adam touched her hand briefly, which made her turn around and face him. They stared at each other for a second. 'Come here,' he placed his hands on her small shoulders and embraced her in a tight hug. She hesitated for a brief moment, but then her arms followed. The bell rang in the corridor making her jump on her spot. She pushed herself away and wiped her tears.

'Thank you,' she whispered and walked off, but this time Adam didn't follow.

Greg met with Adam after school and offered to walk with him as they lived quite close to each other.

'What did everyone say about me?' Adam asked, his hands deep in his pockets, his eyes looking at the houses around him.

'Well, you know, the usual. Some people tried to say that Derek broke your nose or something, but I was there and I saw everything so I knew it wasn't true. A lot of people cheered you every time someone mentioned your name 'cause, as you can see, that guy has a lot of enemies at school. He's a bully, he deserved what came for him,' Greg's voice was energetic. 'I was in your shoes last year, you know.' Adam looked at him, confused. 'My parents moved to Stonebrake from Seattle. My dad got a new job at Stonebrake Hospital. Dean and Joel just came out of nowhere, and then I met Lara. So when I heard about the new guy in school I wanted to make sure you wouldn't be alone,' he sounded truthful and honest. 'Where did you move from?' he asked.

Adam was tense. 'New York.' He hesitated whether he should keep talking, but decided it's only fair that he shares too. 'My grandmother passed away last year and then my mom wanted to move here and take over her shop or something.' He felt weirdly free.

They stopped in front of Greg's house. A big yellow house at least three floors big, was hidden behind huge old oak trees.

'I'm here,' he said. 'Listen, there's a party tonight, the guy is really cool, half the school is probably going, you should too. Give me your number, Dean and Lara will pick me up and we can take you too.'

Before truly thinking about it, he mumbled, 'Cool.' He took his phone out. Wrote down Greg's number and went home.

Adam didn't remember the last time he went to a party. It was at least a year ago. He couldn't remember where it was or who he was with. He was so nervous he was sweating. His anxiety took over. He put on a plain white shirt, threw on some black jeans and, at the last moment, he decided to take Margo's car.

'I'm coming in my car, I will meet you there,' he texted Greg.

He got in the car and the thoughts of Heather rushed into his head. Would she be there? Would she be alone? Maybe she won't come. I wish she would.

Adam found himself in front of a big house. People were already half-drunk, a bunch of people were talking loudly outside on the lawn, some were making out on the porch, or randomly dancing. Loud music was coming from inside. He was surprised that the police hadn't shown up yet. Hesitatingly, he stepped inside the house and looked around. So many people he didn't know. A light tap on his shoulder made him jump. He recognized the girl from earlier.

'Lara,' He smiled. Greg showed up next to her and fist-bumped Adam.

The night flew by so fast. People became drunker and drunker. Adam wanted to leave now, but then he saw her. Her black hair was in a high ponytail and she was wearing her black winter coat. She was holding a plastic cup while drinking slowly from it, her face was somehow sad, irritated even. He noticed a guy talking to her. He was angry and almost screaming at her, but she was unfazed by it. Like she was used to it. Greg pushed another cup of beer in his hand and, by the time he turned around to look at Heather, she was nowhere to be found.

'I'm gonna go, do you want a lift home?' Adam asked Lara, who was the only sober person amongst his friends, who reassured him she would drive them home soon, so he left.

'I'm tired of your bullshit,' someone shouted. He kept walking towards his car when he heard her voice.

'You're drunk, Zack. Leave me alone,' Heather's voice sounded scared.

'Heather!' Adam shouted. Zack's hands were holding her wrists tightly. 'Let her go.' His voice was serious and angry. Zack did that but turned around and faced Adam.

'Get in my car,' He continued. Heather was clutching her bag hard and walked behind Adam's body.

'And who the hell are you, big guy?' Zack said, coming closer and closer towards his face.

'You touch her again and I will smash your face to the ground.' His hands were in tight fists, but there was something in his eyes that scared Zack, so he stepped back while they walked away.

Everyone was already asleep. The only light was coming from a little corridor between the kitchen and the living room. He pointed towards his room and she followed.

'You can grab the bed, I will take the floor,' he said. She didn't say much, but her body was shaking. Was she afraid or maybe it was the cold?!

Adam tried to fall asleep, but he struggled. He couldn't stop thinking about tonight. What if he'd hit her? Had he hit her before?

'Are you asleep?' a whisper broke his thoughts.

'No,' he replied.

'He never hit me. He just gets a bit rough when he's drinking, but he's a good guy,' she said as if she read his mind. Adam didn't reply, he wasn't sure what to say anyway. 'Thank you.'

'Yeah, no worries,' he replied, not sure how exactly he really felt.

8.

'Kyle, just the person I was looking for.'

'Sean, what's going on?' Kyle asked, surprised. He poured himself a cup of coffee and grabbed his backpack.

'Well, as you know it's Friday and me and some other teachers have decided to go for drinks after work. Why don't you join us? I think it would be nice to get to know each other a bit better.'

Sean Arthur was the biology teacher. He was in his mid-forties, a very skinny and short guy, but everyone loved him. Kyle found him very awkward to talk to, so most of the time he ignored him.

'Well, you know I have had a long day, so I might just head home,' Kyle tried to leave, but Sean was not moving out of his way.

'I think it would be great if you came.' Kyle knew he had to say yes or else Sean wouldn't move. He agreed to one drink and walked away as fast as he could.

The bar they met was approximately a thirty-minute walk from the school, so he met Adam before leaving and gave him the keys for his car to drive it home and he would grab a cab after.

Through the glass door, he recognized Eleanor who was excitingly chatting with another woman, who Kyle remembered vaguely but, apparently, she knew him as she approached him by his first name a couple of times. He enjoyed the company of the other teachers and he was nicely surprised to see that Eleanor couldn't stop looking at him. After way too many bears, she offered him to go for a smoke outside. He followed her and stood in the cold and fresh air outside. He noticed that Eleanor couldn't stand straight, but he knew he was more drunk than her. He took the cigarette and lit it.

'Didn't imagine you smoke,' he said.

'Just sometimes after a long day or if I'm drinking.'

Before he knew it, her hands touched his jacket. He felt the attraction between them like electricity. He pulled her body towards him and kissed her. 'Do you want to go to mine?' she asked, holding tight onto him.

'Yes,' he replied without thinking twice.

Her apartment was full of books. It was one bedroom with a beautiful balcony view. His fingers touched her hair and she felt his other hand going under her shirt. She removed his jacket and then his shirt. The lights stayed off, there were clothes everywhere.

'Are you sure about this?' he whispered, out of breath. Instead of replying, her lips kissed his neck again and again. He removed her shirt and stopped at her pink bra.

'That's cute,' he laughed and then removed it.

She felt so soft, like sand in the summertime, so he embraced it all without thinking about tomorrow.

The February sun covered the small apartment in gold light. Kyle woke up and looked around.

The bedroom was small and tidy, it had different pictures and small paintings hanging on the walls. Everything from last night started coming back and his eyes started looking for her.

'Hey, sleepy head,' her voice echoed in his chest. She stood tall next to the door holding a boiling cup of coffee. He recognized his black shirt on her body. He put his hands behind his neck and stared at her.

'Well, where's my coffee?' he said boldly. She laughed and left the room. He stood up and followed her. The kitchen was in dark green colors. She filled a white cup with coffee and placed it in his hands.

'I had fun last night,' she said. Her back was now resting on the kitchen counter.

'Me too,' he replied and kissed her. She pushed him gently and smiled.

'Don't you think you have to ask me out on a date before kissing me again?' she asked, her face serious.

'I think it's a bit late for that!' He laughed and kissed her again. 'But if you insist… ' He placed another kiss on her shoulder. 'Would you like to grab a coffee like right now, because… unfortunately, you make terrible coffee.' She pushed him and laughed loudly.

'So cheeky.'

Nefeli's was a small diner under Eleanor's building. It was a Greek diner that was open twenty-four-seven. It was owned by a very big Greek family back in the 1960s.

'Apparently, people from the Mafia used to come here when it first opened,' Eleanor explained and opened the door. Kyle who grew up in this city knew every inch of it; he had heard of this place but had never visited. It was ten in the morning, but the little restaurant was almost full to the brim.

'Elle. Welcome, my child,' a woman with a thick accent shouted. She hugged her and then looked at Kyle. 'And who is this?' she asked, surprised.

'Calliope, this is Kyle. Kyle, this is the owner's wife, Calliope,' she introduced them. Calli was a big woman, tall and strongly built. She shouted something in Greek and, out of nowhere, another woman showed up. She was quite short but very skinny. Her hair was in a big, tight bun. She said something that Kyle didn't understand and hugged them a bit too tight.

'This is Alejandra, Calliope's older sister,' Eleanor whispered. The women walked them to a table in the far corner and sat them down.

'Coffee?' Calliope asked.

'Two, please,' Eleanor ordered and the woman disappeared.

'So, I'm guessing you're a regular here?' Kyle asked and looked around the place.

'I am or at least used to be. When I first moved here I had problems sleeping so I would just hang here. They are an absolutely amazing family. So funny and caring,' she explained. Kyle stared at her face. Her pale skin was glowing, her bright blue eyes shining. She took a sip of her coffee and smiled.

'Do you have a family?' her eyes were curious.

'I have an older sister, a nephew and a niece. I live with them,' he said. 'This coffee is amazing,' he took another sip. 'I haven't been married nor have kids, if that's what you're asking.'

'I was,' she said calmly. Kyle left the cup on the table, puzzled. 'Married. It was a long time ago.'

'I will need a bit more information,' he said.

She laughed at him. 'I was twenty-one, we'd known each other since we were fourteen. The marriage didn't work out in the end. He wasn't made to be a father,' she explained.

'Well, we have more in common than I thought then. I almost became a dad, but my ex had an abortion behind my back and then changed her address, phone number and job. I guess she dumped me in her own way.' This time his laugh was a bit sad, painful. Eleanor took his hand in hers.

'You need to forgive her, if not, you will lead a very sad life.'

9.

Days turned into weeks, and March already rolled in with full force. The diner was almost done and Margo's favorite burgundy chairs finally arrived.

'Wow… it looks so much better than in my head.' Evelyn laughed. She moved her hand across the mahogany countertop.

'Gorgeous,' she whispered. 'I'm really proud of you. Your mum and dad would be bursting with joy if they were here.'

'Thank you,' Margo replied. 'The coffee machine was installed earlier, wanna try?'

'So New York, huh… do you think that is a wise idea?' Evie took a hesitant sip from her cup and smiled, surprised. 'That's some good coffee.'

'I told you about Adam and Victor right? Well, Victor texted him back, inviting him to New York for spring break. I can't really tell you how Heather got involved, but those two have been spending a lot of time together for the past month.' Margo's eyebrow went up in amusement.

'She claims they are JUST friends, but she and Zack are not together anymore.' Gossip was always their favorite talks and sometimes it felt like their conversations didn't have an end or direction for that matter.

'They will go for the weekend and will stay in our old house and they will be okay. They needt his trip or maybe we do... you know we have to get used to them being away,' Margo smiled sadly.

'Okay, I trust Adam, he's a nice boy. God, when did they grow up? What's next? Grandkids?' They laughed it off but, deep down, both hoped that wouldn't happen anywhere in the near-future.

Margo's phone vibrated in her pocket. Luke. She smiled without realizing, but didn't pick up.

'Why didn't you pick it up?' Evie asked, confused.

'Because I'm with you, he can wait,' she laughed. Her phone rang again, this time it was an unknown number.

'I think you should take this one.'

'Hello?' her voice was a bit shaky now.

'Hello, I am looking for Margo Hunter?' a steady male voice said.

'Yes?'

'I'm calling from the NYPD, we are calling regarding Gavin Hunter, ma'am. Unfortunately, your ex husband was found dead in his apartment this morning. We are very sorry for your loss.'

Margo's heart sank. She wasn't sure how to feel. Relieved? Sad? Scared? What was she going to say to their kids? Did his parents know?

'Margo?' Evie's voice echoed. 'Margo! What happened?' She turned around to face her friend.

Her face was so pale.

'Gavin is... dead,' she whispered.

'Oh, my God!' Evie sat Margo on the nearest chair and poured her a glass of water, her arms shaking a bit.

Luke kept calling, but Margo didn't have the heart to pick up. Not yet. Adam came in later that evening. His mood had changed drastically in the last month and she loved seeing him so happy.

'Hey, honey. Come here.' She pointed towards the empty spot on the sofa. 'I have some news,' her voice changed. Sadness crept behind it.

'Is this about New York? Did Evie say no about Heather?' he tried guessing.

'No, no... it's about your dad. Honey... he was found dead this morning.' Her hand held his tightly.

'Oh.' Silence took over once again. 'He's gone?'

She shook her head.

'It's okay to be sad, Adam. Even after everything that happened, it's okay to feel mournful, no matter what kind of person he was, he was still your dad and he still loved you, even though he was troubled.'

'Yeah... ' He lay his head on her shoulder. Just sitting in silence. 'Did you tell Rose?' his voice asked.

'Not yet. I couldn't bring myself to do it yet.'

'Let me,' he replied calmly.

Adam stood tall and disappeared. The doorbell made Margo jump in her place. It was Luke.

'Hey,' she tried smiling, but she let herself get lost in his embrace instead. A single tear fell down her face.

After telling him about Gavin they sat down on the porch steps. The night sky was their only light. He was holding her tight and even the silence felt comfortable.

'How do you feel?' he finally spoke.

'I... pity him. He used to be a good man. I hate how he ruined his life. And I hate myself for this.'

She placed her hands on her face. 'Am I a bad person for feeling that way?' she whispered.

'No. You're just a normal person, who got so hurt by this man that the fact you feel something other than joy is weird for most people.'

She laughed and looked up at him. She took his face and kissed him. She wanted to do this for so long, but she couldn't bring herself to do it.

'Thank you,' she said. 'For being here.'

His fingers touched her red cheeks. 'Always,' he replied.

***

After Luke left, she went upstairs to check on Rose and Adam. To her surprise, she found them already asleep. Rose's little body was in a ball cuddled next to Adam. She stood there watching them for a bit.

'Come back, stay for the night,' she texted Luke.

'Somehow I knew you would say that, I'm still in front,' he replied.

She opened the door and they quietly sneaked into her room. The lights were out and the cold breeze from the open window was a welcomed friend.

'Are you sure about this?' he whispered, tracing his fingers on her body.

'More than anything right now.' She removed her sweater and let it fall on the ground. She put her arms around him, letting him take over her. Trusting him with every step. Letting him see her truly in a way she couldn't let anyone else see her. His jacket fell next to her sweater, followed by his shirt. Her skin was burning with every touch. His hands were firm but gentle.

They lay down on the bed and the last thing Margo saw was the painting on the wall of a girl with a red veil and then her eyes closed, leaving the moment to take control.

10.

The world felt still. Caved in. Adam felt so many emotions for the past couple of weeks. They decided not to go to the funeral last Sunday. His grandparents were the only people there.

He felt guilt, a solid rock in his chest.

'I know he loved you all so much, even though he made terrible mistakes,' his grandmother told him on the phone. Mistakes. That word echoed in his head since.

'Hey, you have a guest,' Margo's voice interrupted his train of thought. He looked up and saw Heather smiling. She sat close to him on the bed, his hand found hers. She grabbed it and lay down next to him, his face facing hers. Their hands not letting go of each other.

'How are you?' she asked.

'I don't know how I feel and I hate that everyone is asking me how I am. I don't know, I wish I did but I don't. He was my dad, he was a fuck up from every side, but I still remember how he played football with me in the backyard when I was trying for the team. How he would take me early from school and go for ice cream without telling mum. And then I remember the fights between him and mum and how I would hold Rose in my arms for hours just so she can fall asleep and not be scared. Then I remember what he did to them and it makes me feel angry but sad. I pity him, I pity him because he died alone with his mistakes. And I should say he deserved it but he didn't. Because he was a good man inside, but with a broken mind and heart.'

There was a silence between them, but it didn't feel heavy, it felt somehow needed.

'Do you know what he did?' he asked.

'No, mom never told me,' she replied, her voice was balanced.

He thought about it for a minute, letting himself remember.

'I was with Victor that day, we skipped school and stayed home to play some stupid video game.

I don't even remember how long we were playing before my mom called me. Shouting something about Rose. He took her early from school and drove off without telling anyone.

Victor and I went to look for them, he went to his apartment which is such a stupid place to hide,' he chuckled. Heather gripped his hand harder, anticipating what was to come. 'He was so drunk at this point, he could barely stand straight. Rose was so scared, she was in tears and she never cried, even when she was a baby. He tried to stop me, but I pushed him. Instead of taking Rose and leaving, I told Victor to take her and I took the baseball bat that was next to the door and I started hitting him.' His body started trembling and tears rushed down his face. 'He was a drunk, a man who I once called dad. The bat fell to the ground at some point so I started hitting him with my hands. I didn't feel pain, I felt anger and that was it. Most people don't remember much when they fall into that hole, but I do. Every punch, every helpless cry from him I remember. Victor tried to stop me, but I pushed him and I punched him so hard, his nose started bleeding. "Don't fucking touch me," I told him. Mom was waiting outside with Rose, she almost lost it when she saw me. I just walked off, no idea where.'

'Adam,' Heather's voice broke down. Their bodies were closer, she could feel his pain.

'The first thing I told her when I came home that night was, "I think I killed him, I'm not sure if he was breathing."And now he's dead and, I shouldn't, but I feel sad and I don't know how to stop that feeling.' His tears were falling, making it hard for him to breathe. Heather hugged him as he crumpled into a ball, helplessly. Incapable of moving.

Adam wanted to cancel the trip to New York the following week, but Heather didn't let him.

The cab stopped in front of his old home. Nothing had changed, the old tree on the sidewalk was still there, people rushing for work didn't even know the house had been empty for months now. A nostalgic feeling took over him. He opened the door and looked around. Most of the furniture was covered with what were once white sheets, now they were more like a yellowish color.

'Such a gorgeous house, who would've thought it's hidden here like that.' Heather kept looking around. 'Good thing, Margo decided to keep it instead of selling it.'

'She wanted to, but we decided to keep it for when I move here for university,' Adam explained and removed the sheet from the sofa. Still, the same dark green couch as he remembered it.

'Oh, you haven't mentioned you wanted to move back here,' Heather said, surprised.

'Hm,' he wanted to avoid this subject as much as possible. 'It's currently eight-twenty-three a.m. Do you want to have a nap or go for breakfast?' he smiled.

'Breakfast,' she replied while yawning loudly. 'After a nap,' she laughed.

'I looked up at the sky and prayed. I wasn't a believer but, at this moment, I was willing. I would sacrifice myself If I have to, just so I can see you again. Every second of every minute I crave you, I crave your lips, your touch, your neck. I swear at this moment I was willing to believe in every God that ever existed on this planet, just so I can see you even for a second.' Adam closed the book, somehow without realizing this little text resonated on a level he didn't know was possible. He left the book on its spot and looked around for her. She was standing close to the door, turning the pages of a forgotten book of sonnets.

Her dark hair shone under the sunset.

He looked at his watch, Victor should probably be here already.

'Is it time?' she asked.

'I think so, although he hasn't texted yet.'

'Hm, maybe you go and I will stay here, call me when you're ready.'

He exited the bookshop and started walking towards the park where he and Victor would hang out. He knew this path so well, he'd walked it so many times but, for the first time, he felt so nervous, scared even. The last time he saw him he told him he didn't want to see him again and who could blame him? 'I have known you for thirteen years and this is the first time you scared me like that,' he told him. 'I don't think I can be your friend anymore.'

Victor was sitting on a big rock in the middle of Hyde Park. He stood tall when he saw him.

Adam was unsure of what to do so he just mumbled, 'Hey,' waiting for some kind of response. In a way he received it but not in the way he imagined. Victor hugged him. A tight hug. Probably the first time they actually hugged like that.

'I missed you, man,' Victor said and took a step back grinning.

'I missed you too,' he laughed.

'I'm sorry about your dad. He was an asshole though.' Victor always spoke his mind, no matter the situation. For someone else hearing this, they would get angry or even sad but Adam laughed. For the first time in weeks, he finally heard the words he couldn't bring himself to say,

'I'm really happy to see you! How have you been? How's school?' They sat on a bench and talked for what felt like forever.

Heather found them later and met the infamous Victor, whom Adam couldn't stop talking about for the whole trip to New York.

'I have heard so many stories about you, I feel like I know you already,' she smiled.

'Listen, there's a party later today. I spoke with Nathan and Dan, they can't wait to see you. You two should come.'

Adam looked at Heather, letting her decide.

'Or if you don't want to, we can do something else,' Victor continued.

'I was always curious how you New Yorkers party, why not!' Heather interrupted him, and Adam just laughed.

'Party it is then,' Victor clapped approvingly.

The party was in a really expensive area in New York, the house was massive.

'It looks like something out of Gossip Girl,' Heather said.

People were going in and just getting lost. The ground was vibrating from the music. People were dancing and drunkenly making out with people they probably didn't know. Adam took Heather's hand while moving in front of her towards the bar where the crowd was significantly smaller, but he didn't let go of her arm, he was holding it even tighter.

'Wow, good thing I went for a dress then, everyone looks so fancy,' she pointed out.

'You wanted to see how we party, little girl. This is it.' Victor gave her a glass full of something that smelled like watermelon.

'ADAM BOY!' a voice screamed in the distance.

'Nate!' Without realizing, he let go of Heather's hand and hugged a boy who was at least a head smaller than him. His long blonde hair was in a small bun, covered in glitter. 'Is that... DAN!' Another guy appeared next to them out of thin air. He was taller than Adam, his shirt was ripped on more than 3 spots on the front, definitely not on purpose.

'What happened to you?' Adam pointed at his grey shirt.

'A guy tried to fight with me, man. This was my favorite shirt you know. Oh, Amber is here, I just saw her.' Dan's face became a huge grin, his eyebrows raised high.

Adam looked around and saw Heather sitting awkwardly behind him. 'Hey,' he shouted at her and pushed her in front of him.

'This is Heather, one of THE best friends I have,' he introduced her. She looked at him puzzled.

Dan and Nathan started joking around with her and she just went along. Victor took Adam to the side.

'Let's move away from Amber, man, she became awful after you left,' his look went towards Heather. 'If she sees you with her, she will drag her out of here.'

'Amber?' Adam replied, surprised.

'Like I said, she changed.' Victor patted him on the back and went back to his friends.

Victor kept dancing with Heather for most of the night making sure to keep his hands away from her. He wasn't stupid, he knew too well who Heather was.

'She looks cool,' Dan smiled at Adam. 'Victor mentioned that you might be coming back to New York, man. That's amazing. Can't wait to have you full time,' he laughed loudly.

After coming home, Adam could barely feel his feet.

'Did you enjoy yourself?' he asked her.

'Yeah! Your friends are amazing and hands down to Victor, the best dance partner I have had.'

She sat on top of the kitchen counter and took a sip from her glass of water. 'Who's Amber? I heard you and Victor mentioning her a couple of times,' she asked out of nowhere.

Adam stopped in his place. 'My ex.'

'Oh.' An awkward silence took its place in the air.

'Am I really just a friend to you?' her voice was unsure.

'Well, you are,' he replied, he felt a burning desire to tell her so many things, but he was afraid she would say it was the alcohol talking, so he didn't.

'What do you want from me Adam?' her voice was steady, wanting more, longing for more.

He looked at her, breathed her face and her lips, her tiny waist and perfect neck.

'I want you. I want all of you, that's what I'm sure of. And the only thing that I am one hundred percent sure of in my pathetic life I can't have. I can't stand the fact that someone else has you, kisses you, hugs you. And it physically hurts me every time I see you with him. I don't even know why you're still him.' So many feelings were flowing in the air between them.

'I broke up with him, I wasn't sure how to tell you,' her voice was more like a whisper, she tried to catch his hand in hers, to feel his hot skin on hers. But there was no one. His hands were in tight fists glued to his body.

He looked at her one last time. Her eyes were painfully beautiful, her hair gracefully falling on her tired shoulders. She wanted him, but maybe it was too late. He smiled and turned around.

His pace was fast and uncontrollable. His fear was that he would turn around and go back to her and he was right.

'Adam.' His name echoed in the kitchen. He stopped in his tracks and as he turned around but all he could feel were her lips on his, her hands on his neck. And it felt right. He finally felt complete.

'I want you too,' she said, barely breathing.

'Then you can have me,' he replied and continued kissing her lips and neck as if his life depended on it.

The next morning, Adam wanted to visit his dad's grave, but his body was shaking. What was he supposed to do? Was it even right? He looked at Heather who was still sleeping next to him. She was his anchor. With her he felt he could do anything.

Adam parked the rented car in front of the gate of the Calvary Cemetery in Queens. The day was cold, but the sun was shining brightly, giving you a warm feeling somewhere inside your body.

They walked for at least twenty minutes until they reached it. It was between two graves that were long-forgotten by their families, if there were any. Heather placed the white roses gently next to the gravestone and her arm brushed through the engraved name, 'Gavin Joseph Hunter'.

'I will give you a second,' she mumbled and walked away, leaving Adam staring down at his shoes. His hands were deep inside his pockets.

'Quite cold today, huh,' he said finally. His body was glued to the ground, not letting him move anywhere closer to the grave. 'I thought I... I don't even know what to say,' he laughed more to himself. 'Rose told me to say hello from her.' He felt ridiculous now. 'I'm sorry, dad. I forgive you!' He felt hot, boiling tears pushing to come out, so he brushed them off and walked off as quickly as he could.

11.

The 6th of April has always been a painful date for Kyle. The day his ex had an abortion with the kid he never knew he had. Sometimes he would catch himself daydreaming of another life. A life that could've been. Thalia was always a bit knocked up in the head, since she was a baby.

Apparently, her mom fell down the stairs while holding her when she was no more than four months old. He never knew when she was joking or when she was angry. She was always ready to party and that was the only true thing he knew about her. Popping drugs and drinking excessive amounts of alcohol were always a must. The funny part was Kyle used to be the same, once upon a time. True party animal. But then he graduated from university and found a stable job, rented a decent apartment in Brooklyn and said stop to everything. He tried to change her for the better, he really did try. He paid for many therapist sessions and sober houses, but when a person doesn't want to change, nothing can make them. The baby was her last chance at redemption.

She even thought about keeping it, but she couldn't. She couldn't say no to alcohol, to drugs.

And that's when Kyle gave up on her. After so many breakups between them, it was hard to truly believe he was done with her, so she came back again and again until one day he closed the door right under her nose. And it was hard because he really loved her, it broke a part of him that could never return. A part that would be missing forever. But life moves on and if you don't move on with it, you get stuck and that was the last thing he wanted. To be stuck in a memory that belonged to yesterday.

Kyle opened the fridge door and took the milk out, before pouring it he noticed the date on it which was three days ago.

'I'm gonna do some shopping later today, do you want something specific?' he shouted from the kitchen. 'Eleanor?'

He found her sitting on the bathroom floor, her towel sitting on top of her hair. She looked up at him and, without a word, she pointed at a little stick next to the sink. He looked at it and then at her and then back to the stick.

'It's positive?' he said. Nothing else came out, just that.

'I'm pregnant, Kyle,' she said through tears. He wasn't sure if they were happy or sad, but he sat down next to her on the cold floor and hugged her.

'I don't want to be a single mum,' she muttered.

'You won't be, because I will be here for you every step of the way,' he replied calmly and just like that, the 30th of March became such a different date for him. It had a whole new meaning.

'It's a healthy baby, somewhere between three and four weeks,' the doctor said. Eleanor was holding Kyle's hand so tight, it felt numb. On the drive back home, Eleanor was mainly bubbling about baby toys and car seats.

'Do you think you became pregnant the first time we slept together?' Kyle asked. She stopped and looked at him laughing.

'Maybe, or maybe the second time,' she tried to joke.

'So, we are doing this right?' his voice became serious. 'Together?'

'Of course. Together.' She squeezed his hand nervously. 'Does that make us a couple then?'

Kyle laughed loudly.

'If that doesn't make us a couple, I don't know what will.'

Eleanor fell asleep early. He took his cup, full to the brim with peppermint tea, and went outside on the small balcony. He took out a cigarette from his secret pocket and lit one. His phone started vibrating.

'So?' Margo's voice was anxious. 'What happened?'

'I'm gonna be a dad,' he whispered, but his voice was shaking. Margo breathed out loudly.

'I cannot express how happy this makes me feel. My little brother is going to be a DAD!' Her excitement made Kyle laugh.

'But you can't tell anyone else, okay? You promise?'

'I promise. Wait, not even Evie?'

'Not even Evie. You already promised anyway.'

'Fine, fine. I will keep your secret! Have you talked about where you're gonna live?'

'Not really, I mean I'm still trying to wrap my mind around the idea I'm gonna be a dad in nine months. But everything will come.'

'I noticed the date earlier today. How do you feel?' Margo's lighter made a screeching sound.

'She texted me yesterday you know. Thalia. She said, 'I need to see you.' His voice became soft, painful.

'Oh.' Margo lost her tongue for a couple of seconds. 'Did you reply?'

'No. Should I have?'

'I think only you have an answer to that question, honey.'

After two hours of turning left, right and center in bed, Kyle gave up on sleeping and, as quietly as possible, he moved into the living room. Thalia's message was eating him alive. Margo's words kept echoing in his head. 'Only you have an answer to that question.' But there was nothing that came. Not even a single flying clue. Maybe it was for the best to leave it like that. No reply, no nothing. No more heartaches.

And that's what he did. He deleted her message and removed her number from his phone. And then he slept without waking up for the rest of the night.

12.

She walked slowly, holding the baby tight in her left arm and pushing the pram with her other hand. The baby was quietly looking around with pure interest. She stopped in front of the house and looked around. It was dark outside and the street was poorly lit. She kissed the baby's cheek before putting her down in her pram and covering her little body with a purple blanket. She made sure that the letter was visible. A single tear rolled down her face, she took a deep breath and pressed the bell. By the time the door opened, Thalia was long-gone as if she was never there.

Margo came home as soon as she heard the news. Kyle was sitting in the kitchen, the letter open wide in front of him. Adam was sitting next to him in silence.

'Kyle,' Margo murmured. 'Where is she?'

'She is upstairs, in Rose's room. Sleeping,' Adam responded.

'She was pregnant. This whole time she was pregnant and she lied to me, she broke my heart and left me. God knows if she was on drugs or not, if she is okay or, or… ' His eyes watered and he covered his face with his hands. 'I hope she never comes back and, even if she does, she will never be a part of this baby's life and that's a promise,' his voice was shaking.

Margo and Adam placed their hands around him and embraced him in a tight hug. Margo placed a silent kiss on her little brother's head and held him, just like she had done for him many, many times before.

'We will do this. Together!' she whispered.

'Together,' Adam said.

It was a shock for everyone. Kyle sat Eleanor down and told her the very same night. They cried together, held each other and promised each other to do this together just like when they found out they were expecting a baby together.

'Her name is Lucy,' he said.

'Who would have known that I would have a small family on such short notice,' she laughed.

'I love you, El.'

'I love you too.'

***

Since Luke stayed for the first time in Margo's house, their relationship became somehow stronger, lighter. They started spending more time together, Margo even met his sons, who embraced her with open arms. They hadn't really made it official, but there was no need. Margo opened herself like a book to him and he embraced her in the most beautiful and gentle way. She felt truly happy for the first time in years. She felt like a teenager again, the butterflies in her stomach, that never-ending lust for him. The restaurant was finally finished and tomorrow was the big opening day. She was placing the cups on the top of the coffee machine when he walked in. His white shirt was already covered in dust, his usual green cap was missing which is not something you will see every day.

'Hello, stranger.' She smiled brightly and walked towards him. He pointed towards his clothes signaling he was too dirty to touch her and, instead, gave her a careful kiss on the nose.

'Kyle, Eleanor and Evelyn are coming for dinner tonight, why don't you bring Jamie and Noah if they are free?' she offered.

His face was sad, his eyes were missing their usual spark and she noticed immediately.

Something was wrong.

'I have to tell you something.' His voice was heavy. 'I should've told you earlier… '

'What's going on?'

'It's Lila. You remember I told you that she's been in a hospice for years now… ' Margo's body was shaking, she took hold of the chair next to her trying to hold it together. 'They tried new medicine on her a couple of months ago and she responded very well to it.' Her heart was pounding so hard, it might've been visible through her cardigan. 'They want to send her home, Margo. She's coming home.' He tried to catch her hand, but she moved sharply.

'Oh.' She felt guilty for being angry with him. It wasn't fair she was angry with him, but she couldn't snap out of it. Was he breaking up with her? Were they getting back together?

'When?' she mumbled.

'Monday,' his voice was low now. 'Margo, I have to take her, the boys... It's their mother.'

She fixed her posture, put her head up high and smiled. 'Of course. You should.' She cleared her throat. Instead of butterflies in her stomach there was a black hole now. When she thought she'd finally found love, he slipped through her hands. Heartbreak, sadness, anger. All these feelings were making her sick.

'Please, let's talk this through.'

'I have to... there're things I need to finish before Sunday night. I think you should go,' she turned around, couldn't bear to face him anymore. She felt ashamed of her reaction. The door closed behind her back and the chill breeze gave her goosebumps.

Evelyn placed the grocery bag on top of the kitchen counter and removed her jacket. 'So you're telling me that his ex-wife who was locked up for years in a psych ward and couldn't recognize her own kids half the time is now okay and Luke is getting back with her?' her voice was high pitched, she could barely gasp for air. She removed the blanket from Lucy and took her little body in her arms and started rocking her. 'There's too much going on in this family, no idea how we are all sane at this point,' she laughed.

'They are not back together, Eve.' Margo's eyes were red and tired. She brushed her fingers through her hair. 'She is their mother, he has to take her home. Where else can she go?'

They looked at each other and shook their heads in a sign of understanding. 'I am so tired, Eve.'

'Babe, you need to talk to him. You love each other and that's rare nowadays.'

'It's been a month since we started dating, maybe it's not that deep for him as it is for me.'

'Jesus, you sound like Heather when she has a crush on someone.' Evelyn hugged Margo and removed a strand of hair from her face. 'Speak with him, the sooner the better.' She placed a kiss on her cheek and continued taking out the groceries from the bag.

Kyle and Eleanor came a couple of hours later.

'I cannot accept that! How can you?' Eleanor asked Margo. 'It's proper bullshit.'

'I agree,' Kyle pitched in, while downing his bottle of beer.

The front door opened and closed. Ned's face was all red and sweaty. On his back was Rose, who was laughing.

'Uncle Ned says I'm too old for back rides.'

'Come here you crazy monkey.' Evelyn picked her up and placed her on her lap. Ned planted a kiss on Evelyn and sat on the chair next to her.

'I heard about the Luke situation, I'm really sorry to hear that.' Margo shot a look at Evelyn who tried to ignore it, by playing with Rose.

'Is there a person in this house that you haven't told?' she laughed.

'We are your family, we share everything, ' Kyle said while passing a beer to Ned.

'MOM?' Adam's voice sounded in the corridor.

'KITCHEN!' she yelled in return. Adam and Heather walked hand in hand, their cheeks blushing. They sat between Kyle and Ned. Eleanor was showing Heather the pictures from her ultrasound and was explaining which part was the baby's head. Rose was talking enthusiastically with Adam while cuddling her head into Eve's chest. She looked around the small table that was full of family. Creating new memories and laughing at old ones. She thought about her mom and dad. How if her dad was here he would be telling stories from his years in the army and would have everyone rolling under the table with laughter or if her mom was here she would've made her favorite dessert, the chocolate fudge cake that only she knew how to make.

Very soon this night would be a bittersweet memory too. Soon Adam would move far away, Kyle was already creating a whole new family on his own. And she would have only Rose. The most independent eight-year-old that she knew. Her little baby. She thought about Luke. Sadness ripped through her chest. She missed him so much, but she was too bitter, too proud to call him, to talk it out with him. Oh, how she wished for him to be here, sitting next to her.

The next two weeks went so fast, it felt like minutes rather than days. The first day of opening the diner went brilliantly. She was more busy than she expected. A lot of people knew Margo because of her mom. 'She would be proud of you,' an old lady told her. 'She was always talking about you and your brother and her grandchildren,' another lady said. Margo didn't know them but she trusted their words, they meant so much to her and they didn't even realize it. Her heart skipped a beat every time the door opened and the bell above it rang. No matter how busy she was she would always look up, hopefully. To see his face, his eyes, his mouth saying her name.

But Luke didn't come. The door kept opening, minute after minute, hour after hour and her hope started slipping away. With days running away she stopped looking at the door every time. The third week of the opening started. The business was so good she had to hire a waitress to help her out. She already had her usual customers. Adam walked in at a fast pace avoiding Margo's eyes.

'Sorry, I spilled coffee on my shirt, had to go home and change before coming here,' he said while putting his burgundy apron on.

'It's okay, honey. At least you're here.' She looked at him in expectation. 'Was there any mail?'

'Yep.'

'And?'

He returned the same look, his fingers going through his dark hair. 'I got a letter.'

Margo's body shivered. His university letter. The first one. 'And?'

'I've been too scared to open it.' He took the white envelope from his bag and placed it gently in his mom's hands. 'Open it for me.' She took it without hesitation and started opening the envelope. 'Heather got in. New York.' Margo started reading it, her facial expression was as hard as stone. 'She applied there just ber me and I can't imagine how disappointed she would be if I… '

'You got in,' his mother whispered. Her eyes filled with happy tears. 'Baby, you got in.' She embraced her little boy in a tight hug. His laugh became quieter until it turned into tiny sobs. 'I am so proud of you and the man you have become. My little baby.' They stayed in each other's arms for a long time. Then she sent him to Heather so he could share the happy news with her. 'Don't forget to tell your uncle too. Give him a call later,' she said after him.

It was nine p.m. already. The new waitress, sixteen-year-old Jenny, mopped the floor and left.

Margo poured herself a big cup of coffee and sat on a chair, took off her shoes and massaged her feet. The doorbell rang behind her back.

'Sorry, we're closed,' she said and turned around to face a middle-aged woman with short blonde hair, tucked behind her ears. She was holding her bag tightly, her fingers were red.

'I'm sorry to bother... I am not a customer,' her voice was quiet, scared even.

'Are you okay? Do you need help?' Margo put her shoes back on and stood up, to face the woman.

'I came to talk to Margo, I'm guessing that's you,' she laughed awkwardly. 'My name is Lila.'

The name ripped through her body like a bullet. 'Luke's wife,' she heard herself saying.

'Ex-wife actually. I promise I won't take more than two minutes of your time,' her eyes looked around the diner, making a full circle and landing back on Margo.

'Jamie and Noah told me about you, you have to forgive them for prying. They had good intentions. They told me that Luke split up with you because of me... kind of,' her voice was sweet and gentle.

'I wouldn't use the word 'split'. We were never officially together,' Margo said in return, immediately regretting it.

'Oh... well. I just wanted to let you know that I am leaving Stonebrake. I decided that it's not really fair to put my family in this kind of position. Me and Luke ended years ago, he deserves to find love. And from what I have heard, he definitely did with you.'

Margo was speechless. Her stomach was tight in a ball, almost exploding from nerves.

'Where are you going?'

'My parents live in London and they are more than happy to have me back so I can help them as well and I need help in general,' she tried to joke. 'I'm still fighting with my illness… and I don't want to put my family through this nightmare twice.'

'Oh,' is all that came out of her mouth.

'Anyway, I came to tell you that Luke is a special kind of a man. One in a thousand and if he chose to love you, Margo, you are so very special too,' she smiled, turned around and left, leaving the doorbell to ring twice after her.

Margo sat down, shocked as to what just happened. Did she dream the whole thing? Maybe she was overtired. 'What the hell… '

13.

The next month was more of a blur. Margo was working almost twenty-four-seven in the diner, which was more popular than she expected and when she had any free time, she helped look after baby Lucy. Adam finally graduated from school and was helping in the diner as much as he could. Kyle and Eleanor found a beautiful two-bedroom house that would be ready to move in, in September. They found out the gender of the baby the previous week. Healthy baby boy. The only argument they had was over the name. Was it Spencer or Aron? Either way, Margo was thrilled to meet the little angel.

Although everything was going well and her life finally changed for the better, she couldn't stop looking for Luke. Searching for him every time she would enter a shop or a restaurant. She missed him way too much, but she was scared not to get hurt again. She wasn't sure if he was even in Stonebrake so she kept going. Day by day. Week by week. Her little heart getting more and more attached to him than ever.

'I will stay longer tonight. I need to see if this sink is going to stop leaking. Yes, I have your grandfather's tools with me. Adam, you don't have to come. I won't flood the diner. Go and have fun. It's your graduation party, just make sure you're safe and call a cab after you leave. I love you too, 'bye.'

She left her phone on the counter and sat on the ground where the pipe was. She had absolutely no idea what she was looking for or even which instrument to use. She brushed her fingers through the metal pipe and somehow it exploded. There was water coming from every side. She tried to hold the pipe and stop the water but it was useless. She quickly stood up and ran to her phone. It was pretty late and every possible shop would be closed. She hesitated for a second and then called his number. Her body trembled.

'Margo?' his voice sounded surprised.

'I... I think I flooded the diner, there's water coming from everywhere and I... I didn't know who else to call.'

He laughed. One newly-found favorite sound to her. 'I will be there in twenty minutes.'

She wasn't sure what was more awkward. Seeing him after a month of full silence or calling him because she flooded her own restaurant. The truth was she didn't have much time to contemplate this question because in no more than ten minutes later he was there. Standing tall in front of her.

His green cap on as usual.

'I thought it would be worse,' he said after he had a look at it. Thirty minutes later the leak stopped.

She covered the floor with every single towel she had with her.

'The pipe needs changing obviously. I can swing by tomorrow morning and change it for you,' his eyes were chasing hers.

'You don't have to, I can call someone to come and have a look at it. You already did enough… '

'Don't be silly, I'm free tomorrow anyway.'

'Oh, okay then. Thank you.' They stood in front of each other. Craving their bodies, their heat was making them both sweat. 'Would you like a coffee? It's filtered and probably cold,' She smiled.

'How can I say no?'

He pushed one of the chairs and sat down. Margo passed him a cup and sat opposite him. The silence felt so calm and familiar.

'How have you been?'

'Yeah, good. Busy, but good. Got a couple of new projects lined up. How's Adam?'

'He graduated with fairly good grades and got accepted into Stone Brook University. He and Heather are moving to New York in August.'

'Heather, huh… ' they laughed. She wanted to take his hand in his, but she didn't.

'I know right… Oh, major news. Kyle's ex-girlfriend showed up with a baby, left the baby to Kyle and left. Eleanor found out she's pregnant and they both agreed to raise the babies together as a family.'

Luke was shocked.

'That's massive. Wow. Congratulations to him,' he smiled, his face was visibly tired, but his blue eyes were bright and lit.

'I know Lila was here,' he said straight. 'She told me before she left.' Margo made sure to make a mental note that she was not lying about that.

'Yes. Let's just say it was quite… surprising.' She took a sip of her coffee. It was a bad coffee, she wasn't surprised Luke hadn't touched his. She felt her pack of cigarettes in her pocket. She wanted one so badly right this second.

'I owe you an apology… ' he started.

'No,' she stopped him. 'I owe you an apology. My reaction was so wrong and I regret not reaching out sooner. But I was so scared of being hurt or rejected that I let that fear guide me.'

'I should've been upfront with you from the beginning. I knew that Lila would be able to come home before I even met you, but I didn't expect it to be so soon. I… I didn't expect to meet you. The moment you walked in, in that cafe I knew.' His eyes met hers. His beautiful blue eyes that made her body melt into his. 'I'm really sorry, I should've told you earlier.'

'You placed your family first and I would've done the same. But I need to know that you are all in, because I can't have my heart broken again.'

He leaned towards her and took her cheeks in his hand. 'I'm all yours, Margo.' His lips kissed hers and she knew he belonged to her and she to him. Forever.

At that moment, every ache, every misplaced heartbeat ceased to exist. She felt whole. In his arms, she felt safe. She felt her forever happiness and this time she would hold onto it with every fiber in her body.

'I love you,' she whispered.

'I love you,' he whispered back.

She got an overwhelming feeling of belonging. Belonging somewhere, to someone. To this town, to her big and loud family, to her brother, to her children, to Luke. And she felt happy, she finally felt at peace.

THE END